Ladybird books are widely available, but in case of
difficulty may be ordered by post or telephone from:

Ladybird Books – Cash Sales Department
Littlegate Road Paignton Devon TQ3 3BE
Telephone 0803 554761

A catalogue record for this book is available
from the British Library

Published by Ladybird Books Ltd Loughborough Leicestershire UK

THE TALE OF
MR JEREMY
FISHER™

Kimberly

Based on the original and authorized story
by Beatrix Potter
Ladybird Books in association with Frederick Warne

Ladybird

Mr Jeremy Fisher lived in a damp,
little house amongst the buttercups at
the edge of a pond.

He was quite pleased when he looked
out one day and saw large drops of
rain splashing in the water.

"Ahh! Nice drop of rain. Be good
fishing today, I shouldn't wonder,"
said Mr Jeremy Fisher. "I'll get some
worms and catch a dish of minnows
for my dinner."

So Mr Jeremy Fisher went digging for worms. "If I catch more than five fish, I'll invite my friends Mr Alderman Ptolemy Tortoise and Sir Isaac Newton to dinner," he thought. "The Alderman, however, only eats salad," Mr Jeremy Fisher remembered.

Then Mr Jeremy Fisher gathered up his worms and set off for home.

Back at his house, Mr Jeremy Fisher
put on his mackintosh and a pair of
shiny galoshes. He took his rod and
basket and made his way to the pond
where he kept his boat, which was
round and green and very like the
other lily leaves.

Mr Jeremy Fisher untied the boat, took a reed pole, and pushed the boat out into the water. "I know just the place for minnows," he said.

After a while Mr Jeremy Fisher stuck his pole into the mud and fastened his boat to it.

Mr Jeremy Fisher settled himself cross-legged and arranged his fishing tackle. His rod was a tough stalk of grass, his line was a fine, long, white horse hair. He had the dearest little red float, and he tied a little wriggling worm at the end.

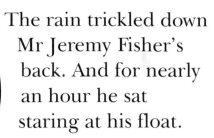

The rain trickled down Mr Jeremy Fisher's back. And for nearly an hour he sat staring at his float.

"This is getting tiresome," sighed Mr Jeremy Fisher. "I foresee, I fear, an adjustment to the dinner menu.

"I'll eat a butterfly sandwich and wait until the shower is over."

Suddenly a great big water-beetle came up underneath the lily leaf and tweaked the toe of one of Mr Jeremy Fisher's galoshes.

"Oh! You beastly creature!" cried Mr Jeremy Fisher. "What a nasty, underhanded thing to do!"

Mr Jeremy Fisher pulled his legs up out of reach, and went on eating his sandwich.

Once or twice Mr Jeremy Fisher
heard something rustling and
splashing amongst the rushes at the
far side of the pond. "Dear me!
I trust that is not a rat," he said. "Oh,
is there no peace to be had anywhere?
I think I had better get away from
here!"

Mr Jeremy Fisher pushed his boat out further into the pond, and dropped some bait into the water. Almost at once his fishing float gave a tremendous bobbit!

"A minnow! A minnow! I have him by the nose!" cried Mr Jeremy Fisher.

Mr Jeremy Fisher jerked up his fishing rod and had a horrible surprise! Instead of a tasty minnow, Mr Jeremy Fisher had caught little Jack Sharp, the stickleback, all covered with spines!

"What are you doing on the end of my line, Jack Sharp?" shouted Mr Jeremy Fisher. "Get off my boat this instant!"

The stickleback floundered about the boat, pricking and snapping at poor Mr Jeremy Fisher. Then Jack Sharp jumped back into the water.

A shoal of little fishes put their heads
out of the water and laughed at
Mr Jeremy Fisher.

"Impertinent little rascals!" he said.

Mr Jeremy Fisher sat on the edge of his boat, waving his sore fingers and peering down into the water. "Oh, what to do! Two such good friends arriving for dinner. One cannot sit them down to butterfly sandwiches!" he sighed. "If only I could remember what I have in the pantry."

While Mr Jeremy Fisher sat thinking,
an enormous trout came leaping up
out of the water.

It seized him with a snap and then it
turned and dived down to the bottom
of the pond! "Ow! Ow! Ow!" cried
Mr Jeremy Fisher in great fright.

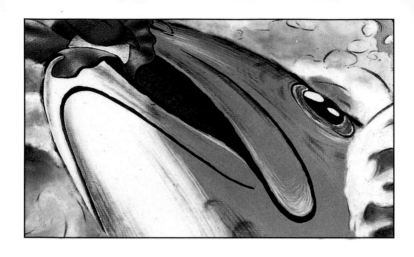

But the trout did not like the taste of Mr Jeremy Fisher's mackintosh. In less than half a minute, it spat him out again. The only things it swallowed were his galoshes.

Mr Jeremy Fisher bounced up to the
surface of the water like a cork and
the bubbles out of a soda bottle.
"Oh! Never, never, have I been so
glad to see the light of day!" he
gasped. "Never has the air smelled
so sweet!"

He swam with all his might to the edge of the pond. "Oh! What a mercy that was not a pike!" he gasped. "My favourite rod! My basket! My only pair of galoshes! Gone! All gone! Oh!

"Though it doesn't much matter," he said, "for I am sure I should never have dared to go fishing again!"

Mr Jeremy Fisher hopped home across the meadow with his mackintosh all in tatters.

He was never so glad to see his house as he was that day!

Mr Jeremy Fisher put some sticking plaster on his fingers, and his friends both came to dinner.

"Good evening, Alderman! Good evening, Sir Isaac!" said Mr Jeremy Fisher.

"Evening, Jeremy, old chap!" said the Alderman.

Sir Isaac Newton wore his very fine
black and gold waistcoat, and
Mr Alderman Ptolemy Tortoise
brought a salad in a string bag,

"But, how kind!" said Mr Jeremy Fisher. "How very thoughtful!"

Mr Jeremy Fisher could not offer his friends fish for dinner, but he had found something else in his pantry.

Instead of a nice dish of minnows, they had roasted grasshopper with ladybird sauce; which frogs consider a beautiful treat!